Billy and Emma

ALICE MEAD

Pictures by
CHRISTY HALE

Farrar Straus Giroux
New York

The author gratefully acknowledges Judy Walker, naturalist,
Maine Audubon Society, for her contribution to the story.

Text copyright © 2000 by Alice Mead
Illustrations copyright © 2000 by Christy Hale
Distributed in Canada by Douglas & McIntyre Ltd.
Color separations by Prestige Graphics
Printed and bound in the United States of America by Worzalla
First edition, 2000

Library of Congress Cataloging-in-Publication Data
Mead, Alice.
    Billy and Emma / Alice Mead ; pictures by Christy Hale. — 1st ed.
      p.   cm.
    Summary: When a robber steals Emma, one of a pair of macaws
  from the zoo, her partner, Billy, sets out to find her with the help
  of some other birds.
    ISBN 0-374-30705-9
    [1. Macaws—Fiction.   2. Birds—Fiction.   3. Zoos—Fiction.]
  I. Hale, Christy, ill.   II. Title.
PZ7.M47887Bi   2000
[E]—dc21   98-49760

To my parents, Dick and Jeanne —A.M.

To my brothers, Jeffrey Sherman Hale
and John Frederick Hale —C.H.

Billy was a blue-gold macaw. Emma was a lovely green. They were best friends, and they lived in a bird cage at the Willowby Zoo.

Next door was a brown spotted owl named Harold. A flock of
gabbling pink flamingos lived in the pond. Nancy, a shiny black
crow, clever bird that she was, didn't live in a cage at all. She
lived in a nest she'd built herself at the top of a tall chestnut tree.

Every day, Harold sat as still as a stump in his cage, waiting to be fed his next dead mouse. The flamingos stood first on one leg, then on the other, and dipped their beaks in the water. On most days, Nancy poked about the zoo with a flock of speckled sparrows. Sometimes she went downtown for lunch.

The macaws, Billy and Emma, did tricks for their snacks. At eleven, two, and four o'clock, they put on a show for the zoo visitors. Wearing a red fireman's hat, Billy climbed a ladder— claw over claw, claw over claw—and rang a bell at the top. Emma bobbed her head five times and kissed herself in the mirror. And they both knew how to talk.

"When do we eat? Let's go. Dinnertime. Monkey chased the weasel. Call the police! Lazy oaf."

Emma even spoke a little Spanish. "Olé! Adiós. Burrito."

For the grand finale of every performance, Emma played a few notes of the *Moonlight Sonata* on a tiny piano. The music never failed to move Billy to tears.

"Pretty bird, pretty bird," he said, and pressed his beak to Emma's.

And so the days passed. Then, one night, when all the birds were sleeping except Harold, who had kept a big yellow eye open, a robber broke into the zoo! He carried a large sack and a flashlight. Silently he tiptoed—past the lions, past the tigers, past the sleeping pink flamingos—to Billy and Emma's cage.

Only Harold was watching as the robber pulled a clipper from his pocket and cut the cage wires, *snip, snip, snip.*

"Hoot!" boomed Harold, sounding his alarm. *"Hoooooot!"*

Emma woke up. "Dinnertime?" she squawked in confusion. "Burrito! Burrito!"

"Fire!" shouted Billy.

They flapped wildly about their cage, trying to escape. With a lunge, the robber grabbed Emma by one wing, pulled her out of the cage, and stuffed her in his sack.

"Lazy oaf! Lazy oaf!" cried Emma from inside the bag, only the sound was muffled by the sack.

"Crahhhk! Crahhhk!" shrieked Nancy, rushing down to help.

She locked her claws in the robber's hair and pecked the top of his head as he ran for the zoo gates. But he managed to throw her off, and escaped.

"Fire! Fire!" Billy called, but no one came.

The next morning, the zookeeper found a sad and lonely Billy in the cage. Emma was gone.

"Monkey chased the weasel," said Billy, and turned his head to the wall. "Bad weasel. Bad, bad."

The zookeeper used a piece of shiny wire to mend the hole the robber had made.

At eleven, two, and four o'clock, the crowd came, but Billy wouldn't perform. The visitors missed Emma, too.

Nancy helped the zookeeper put up posters of Emma all over town. The reward was three rides on a camel.

Day after day went by.

Billy grew sadder and sadder without his friend. He began to molt. His beak peeled, and his beetle-bright eyes turned cloudy with a storm of unshed tears.

No one had seen Emma.

Finally Billy could bear it no longer. He would try to find Emma himself.

"Then I'll go, too," said Nancy.

Harold woke Billy at midnight. Nancy unwound the wire that the zookeeper had used to mend Billy's cage and helped him climb out. He jumped to a bench, then to a branch. He flapped his wings. They were on their way. But Billy's night vision was terrible. He nearly flew smack into a statue.

Billy passed the walrus pen, the camel lot, the snake house, and the zoo gates. Nancy led him downtown as he called, "Emma! Emma!"

Next, they flew across the train tracks and headed uptown. Up and down each and every street they flew, squawking Emma's name and hoping to hear her voice in reply. But all the birds in the city were asleep.

They flew to 116th Street, 148th Street, Barnaby Street, Elm Street. They flew and flew until Billy was exhausted. It was nearly dawn, and they hadn't found Emma.

Worse yet, they were lost. Even clever Nancy didn't know where they were.

"Don't worry," Nancy said. "The pigeons will help us."

Billy perched on a Dumpster next to some puffy-chested homing pigeons. "Have you seen my friend?"

"Who?" they asked. "Who?"

"Her name is Emma. She's a macaw."

The pigeons huddled together. Then, suddenly, they flapped upward, waving their wings for Billy and Nancy to follow them.

The pigeons led Billy and Nancy to a corner rooftop at 113th and Audubon. There they landed and waddled over to the gutter.

"*Coo,*" said the pigeons.

"Emma?" Billy called, his voice shaky and weak. Where was she? He peeked over the edge.

Then he heard something. It was a very faint sound: "When do we eat? When do we eat?"

"It's Emma!" cried Billy.

In a flash, Billy made his way down the fire escape until he was peeking in the open window. There she was—just barely awake—with her head feathers still ruffled from being tucked under her wing.

"Pretty bird, pretty bird!" Billy said softly.

Billy and Emma touched beaks through the wires of the indoor cage. "Let's go," said Emma.

Billy looked at the door of the cage. He called to Nancy for help.

Nancy landed on the window ledge. She let out a big *"Caw!"* when she saw Emma.

In a second, Nancy opened the cage door and Emma was free! Then, with the help of the pigeons, Nancy, Billy, and Emma flew back to the Willowby Zoo, where they were greeted joyfully.

For the two o'clock show, Billy put on his hat and climbed the ladder. Emma bobbed her head five times and kissed herself in the mirror. But when it came time to play the piano, she screeched an earsplitting screech. She had spotted the robber just outside their cage!

With her beak, Emma banged out wrong notes on her piano. *Bing! Bang! Bong! Boing! Bang! Bang!* The visitors held their ears.

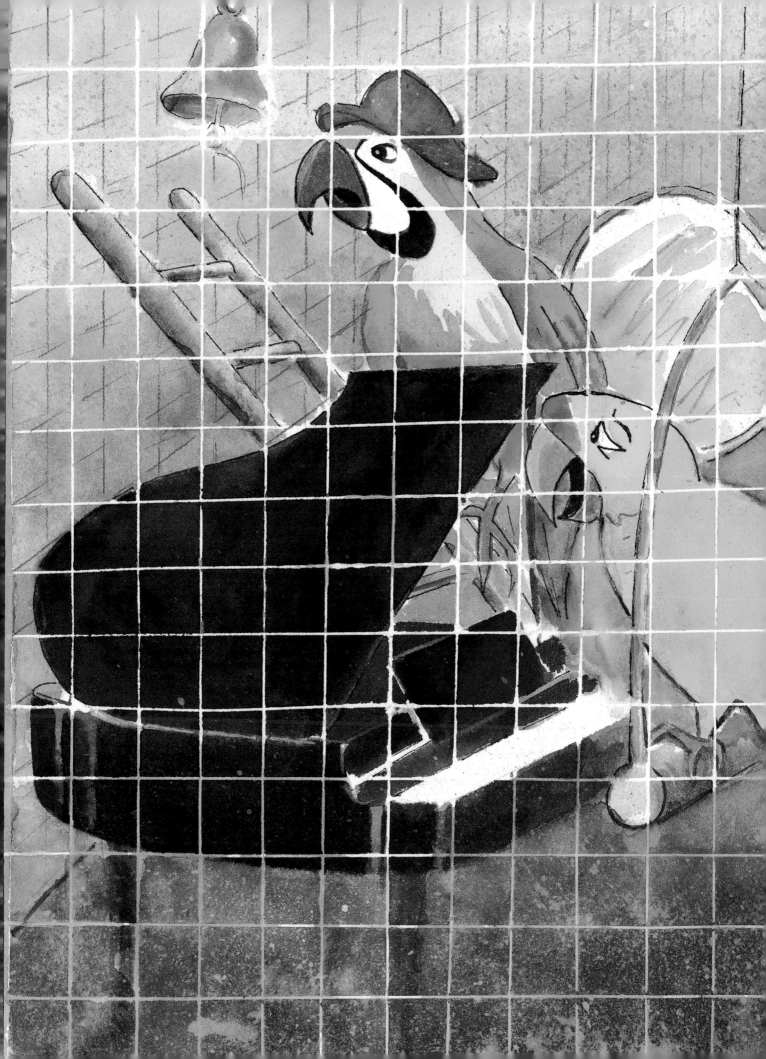

The zookeeper came running. "What's wrong?"

"Call the police!" screeched Emma.

At that, the robber took off running, with Nancy in hot pursuit. Instead of landing on his head, this time she pecked at his shoelaces. She untied them! The robber tripped, stumbled, fell, and plopped into the flamingos' pond.

There the police found him. They put him in handcuffs and led him away.

"Hey!" cried Billy.

"Hey!" cried Emma. "Where's he going?"

Nancy followed the police car.

The robber was taken to a cage for people. He would have to stay there for three whole days.

When Nancy told them, Billy and Emma grumbled. That didn't seem nearly long enough to them.

Nancy explained. "People aren't punished much for hurting birds. Three days will have to do."

To make sure Billy and Emma were safe, the zookeeper put up a poster on their cage. "Notify the zookeeper if you see this man." With the words was a picture of the robber.

The zookeeper was so happy to have Emma back that he bought Billy and Emma new toys. Emma got a music box, and Billy got a hose that actually squirted water, to use in his fireman's act. They had a welcome home party with chunks of fresh fruit.

Billy and Emma were delighted to be back
together. Soon their lives returned to normal,
and the robber never bothered them again.

Author's Note

Scientists are still discovering how smart birds and other animals are.

Macaws, found in Central and South America, love doing tricks. They seem to enjoy music and sway to its rhythms. They have lifelong relationships with their partners. So do swans and geese.

Owls, though long a symbol of wisdom, turn out to be not so clever, after all. But they do have amazing night vision and special soft feathers so that their wings make no noise when they fly.

Crows are good problem-solvers and often alert other animals to danger. They like things that glitter.

Flamingos are wading birds from Mexico and South America. They live in big flocks and gabble constantly.

Pigeons have an incredible ability to navigate. They can find their way home from distances of over six hundred miles. They have been used as messengers since ancient times.